Miss Communication

Random House  New York

Copyright © 2018 by Jennifer Holm and Matthew Holm
Book design by Maria T. Middleton

All rights reserved. Published in the United States by Random House Children's Books, a division of Penguin Random House LLC, New York.

Random House and the colophon are registered trademarks of Penguin Random House LLC.

Visit us on the Web! rhcbooks.com

Educators and librarians, for a variety of teaching tools, visit us at RHTeachersLibrarians.com

Library of Congress Cataloging-in-Publication Data
Names: Holm, Jennifer L., author. | Holm, Matthew, illustrator.
Title: Miss communication / by Jennifer L. Holm and Matthew Holm.
Description: First edition. | New York : Random House, [2018] | Series: Babymouse. Tales from the locker |
Summary: "After finally getting a cell phone, Babymouse tries to increase her popularity in middle school by becoming the queen of social media." —Provided by publisher.
Identifiers: LCCN 2017011512 | ISBN 978-0-399-55441-4 (hardback) | ISBN 978-0-399-55442-1 (glb) | ISBN 978-0-399-55443-8 (epub)
Subjects: | Social media—Fiction. | Cell phones—Fiction. | Popularity—Fiction. | Middle schools—Fiction. | Schools—Fiction. | Mice—Fiction. | Animals—Fiction. | Humorous stories.
Classification: PZ7.H732226 MI 2018 | DDC [Fic]—dc23

Printed in the United States of America
10 9 8 7 6 5 4 3 2 1
First Edition

For Millie, Morgan & Natalie

Contents

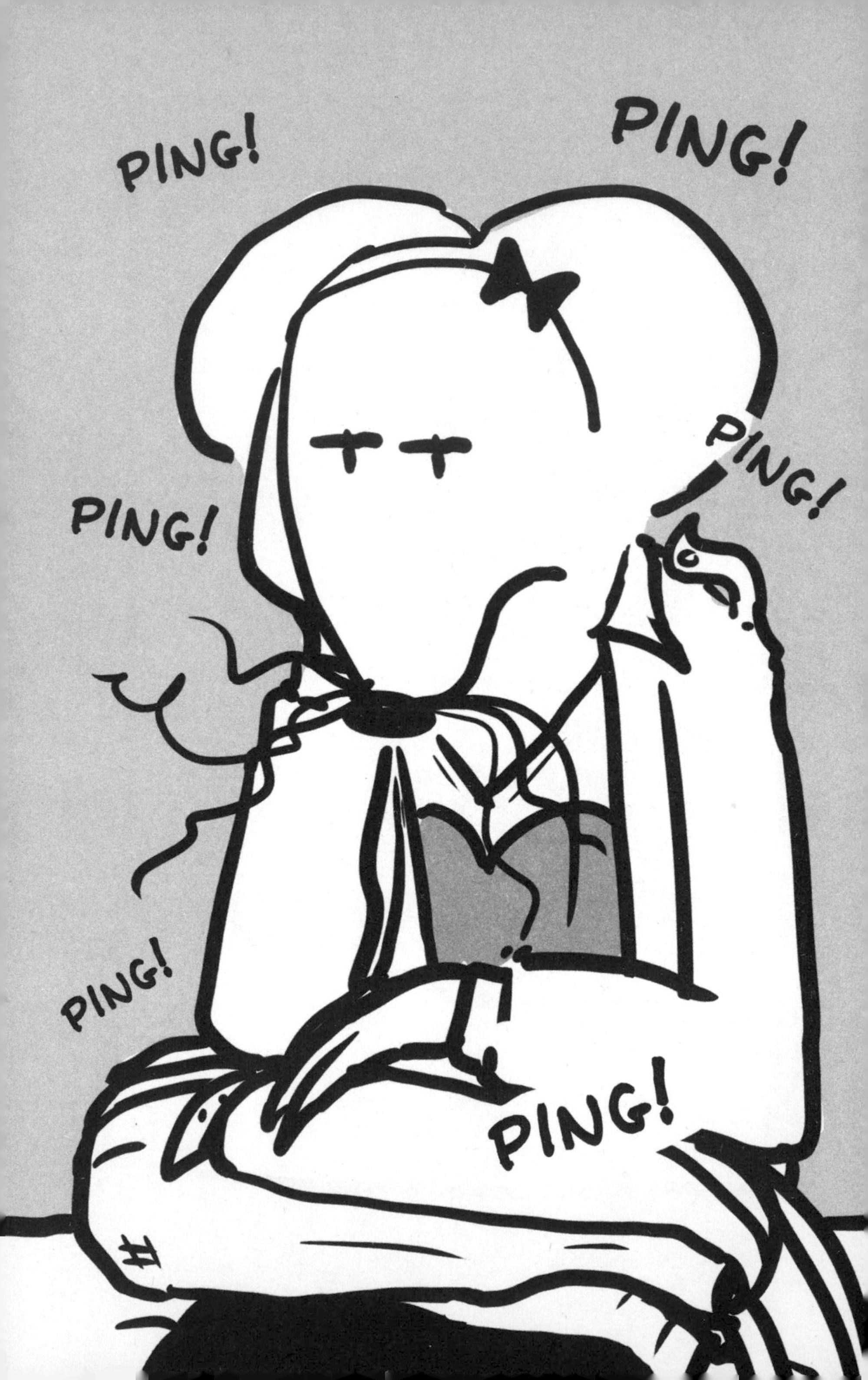
PING!
PING!
PING!
PING!
PING!
PING!

Conversation

So there I was, sitting on the bus on the way to school. And not just any school . . .

MIDDLE SCHOOL.

Dun. Dun. Dun.

I wanted to catch up with my friends, but everywhere I looked, kids were zoned out on their phones. . . .

What was I supposed to do? Twiddle my thumbs?

Le sigh.

Felicia Furrypaws and her crew were sitting in front of me, texting each other. They were laughing hysterically. Why they were texting when they were sitting right next to each other, I couldn't tell you. . . .

I leaned over the back of their seat.

"What's so funny?" I asked.

All four girls stopped texting and looked up from their phones.

"Nothing, Babymouse," Felicia replied coolly.

"None of your business," Melinda added.

"Wouldn't you like to know?" Belinda asked.

"She totally would," Berry answered.

The air filled with laughter—I mean, LOLs.

Hmmph. I slumped back into my seat and wondered what they could be texting about.

Everyone stopped and looked up at me—even the bus driver, who had just pulled up to the school. I could hear crickets chirping outside.

Felicia rolled her eyes. "You are so weird sometimes, Babymouse."

I thought things might get better once I got inside the building, but I was wrong. Kids were walking up and down the hallways texting, not even bothering to look where they were going—which, as it turned out, was almost always directly into ME.

RINGGGG.

I squeaked into homeroom just in time. Mr. Ludwig, my lizard homeroom teacher, didn't even look up from his device. I turned toward my best friend, Wilson. At least **he** would pay attention to me.

"Hey, Wilson," I whispered. "How was your weekend?"

"One sec, Babymouse," he said, putting up a finger. "I just got to the good part!"

Sigh. **Let me know what that feels like,** I thought.

The first class of the day was social studies. I took my seat and pulled out my notebook and a pen.

"Now remember, class," Mr. Gibbons said. "Your reports on ancient Rome are due in a few weeks. As the saying goes, Rome wasn't built in a day, and I hope none of your projects will be, either." He walked up and down the aisles as he spoke.

"I'm sure I don't have to remind you that this assignment makes up eighty percent of your grade, so please do not wait until the last minute."

Mr. Gibbons looked directly at me, though I had no idea why. Okay, maybe I had a **little** hint. Last time we had a huge assignment like this—our ancient Egypt report—I waited until the night before to get started. Well, needless to say, that ended up being a pretty terrible idea, because I had to pull an all-nighter to get it done in time.

Still, I'm not sure how Mr. Gibbons would
have known that. . . .

ZZZZZZ...

I was mostly tuning my teacher out, because it just so happened that I had finished my project early. I really didn't want history to repeat itself (and neither did my parents).

The rest of the day fell as flat as Felicia's pin-straight whiskers. I couldn't strike up a conversation with any of my friends. It seemed like all anyone cared about was updating their statuses, posting selfies, or checking in to different classrooms. With all the checking in, you'd think the school was a hotel.

When I got home, I plopped in front of the TV like a character from one of Wilson's zombie movies. TV made everything better. Usually. But instead, I was taunted by commercial after commercial—every single ad was for the Whiz Bang™ phone!

The Whiz Bang™ jingle was my favorite. I sang along loudly—maybe too loudly, because Mom popped her head in from the other room.

"What is that screeching sound?" she asked. "Is something dying in here?"

"Mom, can I get a cell phone?" I asked.

"You don't need one, Babymouse," she replied.

"But everyone has a cell phone but me!"

"Nobody **needs** a cell phone, Baby-mouse," my mom said. "It's a privilege."

"But what if there's an emergency?"

Mom smiled. "I'll discuss it with your dad and let you know, Babymouse."

Over the next couple of days, I checked in with my parents constantly to see if they had made their decision.

GROCERIES

- milk
- eggs
- apples
- walnuts
- Cell phone for Babymouse ♡

It soon became obvious that begging and pleading were not going to work. So I decided to go in the opposite direction. I gave them the silent treatment.

Unfortunately, they beat me at my own game.

Mom eventually gave me a cupcake, but it came with a lecture.

"You know, Babymouse, if you want to prove to us that you're ready for your own cell phone, you should do it by being more mature, not LESS mature," she said.

That was something I'd never considered before. It almost made sense!

I figured that the best way to prove how responsible I could be was to take really, really good care of a cell-phone-like object for a couple of days. But WHAT?

I scoured my room for anything resembling a cell phone.

But there was nothing that even **remotely** resembled a cell phone. Wait! That was it!

A remote!

I ran into the living room and searched for the TV remote. I eventually found it sandwiched between two couch cushions.

"Mom! Dad!" I yelled. "Come quickly!"

They both came running, thinking it was

an emergency. Which was a good thing, because it pretty much was.

"I have the solution," I proudly told them. "I am going to take excellent care of this remote control for the next couple of days so you can see just how well I am able to care for expensive technology."

My parents looked at each other, unsure. Dad shook his head at Mom, but she raised an eyebrow, and he just sighed. (Parents.)

"Okay, Babymouse," Mom said. "If you can hold on to that remote for the next forty-eight hours without losing or breaking it, we will consider letting you get your own cell phone."

I had this.

☆ ♥ ☆

For the next two days, I didn't let that remote control out of my sight. I even brought it with me to school! (Though I kept it in my locker so people wouldn't think I was weird.) I was also on my best behavior in general. I did my homework without being asked, cleaned up the kitchen, and babysat my brother, Squeak.

That weekend, my parents came into my bedroom, smiling. I was suspicious at first, but then they told me THE. MOST. BABY-MOUSETASTIC. NEWS. EVER.

"We have a surprise for you, Babymouse," Dad said.

"We've decided that you've been very responsible lately," Mom continued.

"And we are willing to let you get your own cell phone on a trial basis, but you have to promise to never use the phone during class," Dad warned.

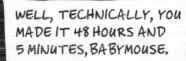

Whiz Bang™

My parents took me to the Whiz Bang™ store.

"Hello. I would like to be a part of the conversation, please," I told the employee at the front desk.

"Huh?" she asked.

"Um, I want to buy a Whiz Bang™ phone, please," I said.

"Oh, okay. Coming right up." She reached down for a tray of display phones and laid them out before me. They sparkled like precious diamonds.

"I'll take that one!" I exclaimed, pointing toward the smallest, coolest one. "It's perfect for me."

"The Whiz Bang™ Mini. Great choice!" the saleswoman said.

"Now, this isn't going to be one of those things where we buy this phone today and the brand-new model comes out tomorrow, is it?" Dad asked.

"Don't worry, sir," she said. "It's very unlikely that that would happen."

She turned her attention back to me. "Have you had a cell phone before?"

"Nope! This is my first one," I replied.

"Congratulations! Just make sure to be very careful with it," she said. "Even with a protective case, the glass screen is very fragile."

"Fragile. Roger that!"

When we got back to the house, Mom and Dad posted a new "Cell Phone Policy" on the fridge.

Cell Phone Policy

1. Communicate with parents at all times.

2. Do not lose phone.

3. Do not drop phone.

4. Do not break phone.

5. Do not talk to strangers.

6. No prank calls.

7. No long-distance calls.

8. No data overages.

9. No using phone during class.

10. ~~shAIYR~~ share with Squeak !!

Even Mom and Dad's strict rules couldn't keep me from being on  9. I was officially part of the conversation (or "convo," as the cool kids called it—I was picking up the lingo already!).

☆ ♥ ☆

The next day, I could hardly wait until lunchtime to show my new phone to my friends. The day dragged on. But finally, the bell rang for lunch!

"Look at my new phone!" I said.

Duckie looked up from a messy PB&J. "Oh. That's a Mini?"

"Uh, yeah?" I responded.

"It's the old model . . . ," Penny said.

The old model? That didn't sound good.

"What do you guys have?" I asked. Everyone held up their phones.

"The new model. The Whiz Bang™ Boom," Wilson said.

Maybe everyone else had the Whiz Bang™ Boom, but that didn't change anything. I still loved my Mini, and it loved me. (Or at least it **would** have if it hadn't been a cell phone.)

I added everyone's information, and made sure to get a pic of each person for their contact profile.

⊕ Contacts

Dad

Duckie

Georgie

Locker

Mom

Penny

Wilson

Now all I needed was Felicia's number. I took a deep breath (of yucky cafeteria air—gross!) and made my way over to the popular table.

"Felicia! Check it out!" I said. "I got a new phone! Can you give me your number?"

Melinda, Belinda, and Berry exchanged smirks.

"A Whiz Bang™ Mini. How precious, Babymouse," Belinda said.

"I didn't even know they made those anymore." Berry added.

"Did you get it at an antiques store?" Melinda asked.

"I, uh, got it at the mall," I stammered. I looked at Felicia and handed her my phone before anyone could say anything else. I was relieved when she took it right away.

"Sure, Babymouse. I'll give you **my** number." She smiled widely.

I was surprised she was being so nice,

but I thought maybe it was because having a cell phone—even a Mini—gave me immediate CGS (Cool Girl Status). I watched as she carefully punched in the numbers.

"Here you go," she said, handing the phone back to me. Just then, the bell rang.

RINGGGG.

Bye, Felicia.

The next class I had was math. I don't hate-hate-hate math, but let's just say we politely agree to disagree. Especially when it comes to answers. 😄

The clock was ticking slowly. I put my phone in my lap so no one could see, and began watching videos of baby koalas. (That should tell you how boring the class was, because koalas sleep at least eighteen hours a day, and they were **still** more exciting than integers.)

Out of the corner of my eye, I saw a foot tapping next to my desk. I looked up to see my math teacher, Ms. Calculate, standing over me. I smiled my most innocent smile, but she shook her head and pointed to a sign in the front of the room.

The next thing I knew, I was in the principal's office.

Typical.

At the end of the day, I went back to the principal's office to get my phone. Luckily, it was easy to find.

LOL!

Okay, so my phone had a huge crack on the screen. But it still worked. Besides, image filters were totally in! I just pretended to be using a giant spider photo filter for everything.

I had to focus on the positive. For example, now that I had a cell phone, I could go to the Coffee Shoppe after school. The Coffee Shoppe was THE place to see and be seen. (I mean—c'mon—they didn't even spell it "Shop." If that's not cool, I don't know what is. . . .)

All the popular middle-school kids went there after class with their friends. They sat at fancy little tables with overstuffed comfy chairs, texting each other and drinking lattes. It was all so very . . . **French.**

But with my Whiz Bang™ Mini, I would be an outsider no more. (Literally!)

I dashed over to Locker, gathered my things, and started to make my way to the Coffee Shoppe. I wanted to make sure I got a good spot for people watching. I was so happy I was tempted to skip the whole way, except I was pretty sure skipping wasn't cool. (Based on the fact that Penny had repeatedly told me so.)

Hmm, that reminded me to check in with Penny.

I was starting to realize emojis were only great for expressing your feelings if your feelings fell into an existing category. That was pretty limiting. If it was up to me, there would be a customized emoji for every-thing!

Bad Whisker Day
Emoji

Need Cupcake
Emoji

No More Homework
Emoji

Pimples Be Gone!
Emoji

When I arrived at the Coffee Shoppe, I quickly got in line. After what seemed like forever (but was probably only about eight minutes), it was my turn to order.

"What can I get you?" Barista asked. Or at least I assumed that was her name because it was written on her name tag.

"I'll have a latte, please," I said.

"What flavor?" she asked. "We have pumpkin, caramel, vanilla, mocha, peppermint. . . ."

"I'll have that."

"Which one? They're all different flavors."

"Um, I'll take all of them."

She punched the order into the cash register. "What size?" she asked.

"Extra large."

"And your name?" Finally, an easy one.

"Babymouse."

"Okay," she said. "That will be twelve seventy-five."

"Wow, that seems like a lot," I replied, surprised.

"It's an extra dollar fifty for every flavor shot, and you got ALL the flavors, so . . . twelve seventy-five."

I searched through my wallet, wondering

if I would have enough. Then I remembered that Mom had given me a twenty-dollar bill to use in case of emergencies. This definitely counted as an emergency.

After I paid, I went to wait on the other side of the counter. A bunch of people from school were already there, including Georgie.

"Hey, Babymouse," he said. "What's up?"

"Hi, Georgie," I said, looking around. "This place is exciting!"

"Kid-size hot chocolate for Tara!" Barista yelled. A young goat took the steaming cup off the counter.

"Petite black coffee for Georgie!" Barista yelled. Georgie took his drink.

"What did you get?" he asked.

"Extra-large pumpkin caramel vanilla mocha peppermint for Babymoose!" Barista yelled.

"That one's mine," I told Georgie.

The XL was huge! And piping hot, too!

"You can use a sleeve," suggested Barista.

That was a good idea! I pulled my shirt-sleeve down so I didn't have to burn my hand. That helped a little.

"No, I mean a **coffee** sleeve," she said, pointing to a bunch of cardboard cutouts nearby. Georgie opened one and slipped it onto my drink for me.

"Thanks!" I said with a laugh.

In the time it took to make my extra-special latte, the place had become packed. There didn't seem to be any seats left! Then I noticed a small table next to the front door. The spot wasn't great, but it was something. Georgie and I plopped our stuff down. I did my best to shield myself from the wind that came gusting in with each new customer . . . and from their enormous bags.

The gusting air actually helped cool my drink pretty quickly, so finally I was ready to take a sip and soak up all the **cool**.

BLECH!

I looked up to see Felicia and her friends laughing at me from a nearby table.

"Leave the latte drinking to the adults, Babymoose." Felicia snickered. I was mortified. Luckily, my phone buzzed just then with a text.

"It's probably a wrong number." Melinda laughed.

"Or her MOM," Belinda added.

I felt my face flush hot as I looked down at my phone.

Le sigh.

MOM

???

MOM It's 🕐 for you to come 🏠 and babysit Squeak.

Oh no I can't see these messages, bad connection I guess.

MOM No problem. I can come to the café and talk to you in person. ☺

Wow! It looks like my service is better now. Be right 🏠.

MOM

"Don't listen to them, Babymouse," Georgie said. "They're just being mean because they think they're better than everyone else."

"Thanks, Georgie," I said. "I do have to run, though. When Penny gets here, can you tell her I had to deal with a family thing?"

"Yeah, of course," he said, giving me a thumbs-up.

I was halfway home when my phone buzzed. It was Penny.

Sry I missed u.
Was running 18.

you ran eighteen miles??

I was running late. C U tom.

who's Tom?

Lolz. Tomorrow.

oh I get it

PS Get this. Everyone was talking about some girl who ordered ALL the flavors for her latte. Can u imagine? LOL!!!!!

what's the difference between LOLZ and LOL?

srsly?

It was then that I realized there was a whole world of abbreviations I knew nothing about. Think of all the time I could save if only I used fewer words and letters! I needed to look up some text-speak resources ASAP! (As soon as possible—that one I knew.)

LIST OF ABBREVIATIONS

BRB:	Be right back
IDK:	I don't know
JK:	Just kidding
K:	Okay
L8R:	Later
LMK:	Let me know
LOL:	Laugh out loud
OTW:	On the way
PLZ:	Please
SRSLY:	Seriously
TBH:	To be honest
TTYL:	Talk to you later

Common Text Message Abbreviations

The next day after school, armed with tons of new abbreviations, I headed back to the Coffee Shoppe.

i'm OTW 2 c u

Kewl. LMK when u get here!

k

& I hope u don't leave b4 I get there like last time 😬.

lol I won't!

Ping!

My cell phone buzzed to alert me I had a new text. I expected it to be Penny, but instead it was "unidentified."

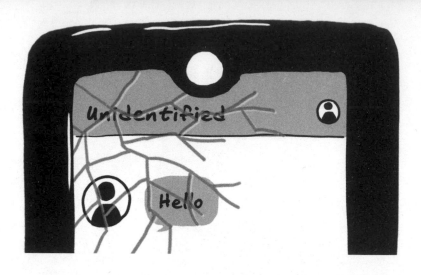

I looked around. The street was completely empty aside from a couple of squirrels. Who was this person texting me? Should I ignore it? I knew that #5 on the list of rules posted on the fridge was "Do not talk to strangers." But (1) texting wasn't TECHNICALLY talking, and (2) I didn't know FOR SURE that the person was a stranger. What if it was one of my friends?

Or maybe a famous director who had seen **Au Revoir, My Locker*** and wanted to offer me a multimillion-dollar blockbuster deal?

*See **Lights, Camera, Middle School!**

I decided to text back to see if I could figure out who it was. After all, millions of dollars may have been at stake!

I was really angry that I had cracked my phone again, but that didn't stop me from going back to the Coffee Shoppe. This time, I made a couple of strategic changes:

1. When I got there, I put my stuff down right away to reserve a good table.
2. Realizing "Barista" was a job title, not a name, I started calling her India. (According to my receipt, that was her name.)
3. To avoid confusion, I S-P-E-L-L-E-D my name out when they asked me for it.
4. I was smart enough to order a single flavor, pumpkin . . . and . . .
5. Only a small size ("petite")—to see if I even liked it!

Penny, Georgie, Wilson, and I sat down at the table I had reserved. Felicia and her friends were loudly gossiping in the corner again, but I was too absorbed in hearing Wilson talk about the latest movie he'd seen to even notice them.

Things were looking up! Maybe, just maybe, I was getting the hang of this middle-school thing after all. 👍

Almost Sorta Barely Famous

It was a day later, and there I was: waiting on the never-ending lunch line in the cafeteria (srsly, why couldn't they just hire more staff?). Felicia and her friends were up ahead, loudly talking about how many followers they had on something called the SoFamous app.

I wasn't surprised that I had never heard

of SoFamous—I was pretty much out of the loop on EVERYTHING—but I was surprised that they weren't freaked out by being "followed," especially since we'd just had that school assembly about "stranger danger."

I decided to look up SoFamous on my phone. It turned out to be a social network that tracked your popularity based on how many people followed you. Back to the present again, I heard Felicia scream dramatically.

"I can't believe it! I just hit ten thousand followers!" she exclaimed.

"No way! You're so famous, Felicia!" replied Melinda.

"World-famous!" said Belinda.

"Galaxy-famous!" Berry added.

Galaxy-famous . . . Wow, I thought.

That would be a dream come true. I could already picture it. . . .

I downloaded the app immediately. When I got to the front of the line, I asked the lunch lady if she wanted to follow me. But she was pretty confused, so I just paid and walked away with my head down, trying not to make a scene.

☆ ♡ ☆

Finally, the last bell of the day rang. I was free to focus on what was important: how to become popular.

On the bus ride home, Felicia plopped down in the seat in back of me.

"How many followers do you have on SoFamous, Babymouse?" she asked.

I looked at my phone. After the reaction from the lunch lady, I hadn't tried to get anyone else to follow me.

"Uh . . ." I pulled up the app, praying that I had miraculously increased in popularity in the last three hours.

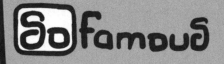

FOLLOWERS: 0

Congratulations, Babymouse! You have "0" followers!

Felicia looked over my shoulder.

"You have NO followers?" she laughed.

"That's like you don't even exist, Babymouse!"

 # KNOW EVERYTHING A PEDIA

Felicia Furrypaws

Felicia Furrypaws is the most popular female middle schooler of all time. She is best known for her strong social-media following, celebrated fashion sense, and perfect score on the National Likability Index.

Felicia Furrypaws, social-media sensation

Furrypaws's dazzling, sparkling personality is adored by all those lucky enough to come into contact with her. She swept into middle school with wit and aplomb, endearing herself to teachers and classmates alike. Her carefully curated wardrobe and no-nonsense attitude make her the envy of all who meet her.

(Last edited yesterday at 4:05 p.m. by user FFFnumeroUno.)

But Felicia was wrong. I existed on the Internet! I knew I did!

So I searched myself.

KNOW EVERYTHING A PEDIA

Babymouse

404 error:

Page not found.

Did you mean "Babymoose"?

Then again, maybe not.

Le sigh.

I was determined to get more followers on SoFamous. I started by friending Gramps—only to find out he had over 400 followers! I sent him a message to see what his secret was.

Well, that was depressing—but still not as depressing as my social status! (Or lack thereof.) There must be a trick to getting followers. I needed to figure it out ASAP.

I texted Wilson.

After school, I followed every cool person I could find. Though my definition of "cool" started to get a little looser after the first hour or so.

So Famous

 Georgie

 Wilson

 Penny

 Duckie

 Locker

 Ms. Octavia

 Mr. Ludwig

 The principal

 The vice principal

 The school nurse

 The school custodian

 The assistant school custodian

 The school crossing guard

All that following became super tedious. After an hour, I only had ten followers! So I decided to bring in reinforcements.

"Hello, favorite brother of mine," I said, with my voice as sweet as a cupcake.

"Only brother of yours," Squeak corrected. "What do you want?"

I cut to the chase.

"I want you to get me as many followers on SoFamous as possible by tomorrow morning," I told him.

Squeak mulled it over. "What's in it for me?" he asked.

"A whole dollar!" I said enthusiastically.

"Five dollars and I'm in," he replied. Talk about supply and demand.

"Fine. But you get half now, and the other half tomorrow morning when I see my spike in popularity," I said, and dug ten quarters out of my change jar.

He nodded and pocketed the coins.

"And no funny business," I warned.

"Funny business," he giggled to himself, in a way that made me a little nervous. He took my phone and disappeared into his room.

The rest of the night, I kicked back and enjoyed myself.

EATING CUPCAKES...

READING...

SLEEPING...

ZZZZZZZZZZZZ...

The next morning, I rolled out of bed, sure
I had risen to stardom overnight. I practiced
a few morning selfie faces in the mirror.

Then I knocked on Squeak's door.

"Do you have it?" I whispered.

"Payment first," he replied. I handed him
the rest of the quarters, and he gave me the
phone.

 **famous**

FOLLOWERS: 9,000

Congratulations, **Babymouse**!
You have "9,000" followers!

I couldn't believe it! I had 9,000 followers! I didn't even know 9,000 people! I couldn't wait to see all my amazing new friends, but I was running late, so I pocketed my phone and rushed out of the house.

At the bus stop, I couldn't contain my happiness. As soon as I saw Felicia, I shouted out the good news.

"Felicia! Guess what?" I cried. "I got nine thousand followers overnight!"

"Let's see," said Felicia.

MR. SQUEAKERS
Occupation:
CLOWN

You are now following:

 Mr. Squeakers

 Saddy McClown

 Boffo the Clown

OH, I GET IT NOW!
#FUNNYBUSINESS

LOL

Picture-Perfect

I couldn't believe it. How embarrassing. I was starting to feel like a clown myself. Did anybody like me? Was I destined to be uncool forever? (Also, I didn't know if I wanted all those creepy clowns following me.)

To Do:

- Pay Squeak $5
  to delete all clowns
  from phone. ☹

Wilson sat down next to me at the lunch table.

"Is everything okay, Babymouse?" he asked. "I feel like you haven't been yourself lately."

I wanted to tell him I'd been so busy worrying about my social status that I wasn't doing much real-life socializing, but instead I just said, "Yeah, everything's fine."

"Just know I'm here if you wanna talk or something."

"Thanks, Wilson," I said.

I guess I should have asked him how everything was going on his end, but I was too busy listening to what was going on at the table next to us. Felicia and her crew were talking about having a professional photo shoot(!) over the weekend so they could get fabulous new profile pics.

This was news to me. People actually got professionals to do personal photo shoots?

I had just taken a screenshot of my fifth-grade school picture from the picture company's website. Sure, it had a "Do Not Copy" watermark, but you could still see my face. (Kinda.)

"I don't know why everyone cares so much about being popular," Wilson said, glancing at Felicia's table. "Isn't it better to just be yourself?"

"Ugh, Wilson. Why would I want to be my actual self when I can be a cooler, more popular version of myself?"

"Why, indeed," he said, shaking his head.

Just then, Penny plopped her tray down next to me.

"Did you guys hear that Felicia and her friends hired a professional photographer to do new profile pics this weekend?"

Wilson did a fake facepalm, then got up to empty his tray. "I'm out."

"Yeah, we were just talking about it!" I replied. "I'm so jealous. I wish I could hire someone to do my picture."

"I can take your picture," Penny offered. "I'm really good at whiskers and makeup, and I know all the good filters to use."

‹ PHOTO FILTERS ›

Vintage

Portrait

Lo-Fi

"You're the best, Penny! Can we do it this weekend?" I asked.

"Sure thing!" she said.

The night before our shoot, I was so excited I could barely sleep. But I had to get my beauty sleep if I wanted to look great the next day. I wondered if Felicia was feeling the same way. She probably was. Maybe she needed someone to talk to, also. Would it be crazy of me to call her? Maybe she would even invite me over for HER photo shoot. I would have to ditch Penny, but she would understand, right? That was what friends were for!

BUT . . .

What if Felicia didn't pick up? Or what if she did pick up and just laughed at me for an hour straight? What if Melinda, Belinda, and Berry were all there for a sleepover, and they all laughed at me for an hour straight? And then what if my parents got mad at me for using all their minutes?!

I couldn't take it anymore! I had to face my fears. I decided to call Felicia.

Her phone rang, and after what seemed like an eternity, someone picked up.

"Hello?" a girl's voice asked.

"Hi! How are you?"

"Good. How can I help you?"

"Well, I'm having trouble falling asleep, so I just wanted to see what you were up to. . . ."

"What I'm up to?" she asked. "I'm working! Is this pickup or delivery?"

"Huh?"

"For the pizzas. Is this pickup or delivery?"

My heart sank.

"Oh, uh, I think I have the wrong number." I immediately hung up.

I couldn't believe it. Felicia had given me a fake number! Srsly????

☆ ♥ ☆

The next morning, I was still bummed, but I'd gotten some sleep and felt better than the night before. The photo shoot would be fun, no matter what.

When I got to Penny's front door, she was already waiting for me.

"Ready for your close-up, dahling?" she asked with a silly accent.

I nodded. I couldn't wait!

"Now, I need to know what kind of image you want to project."

"Image?" I asked.

"You know. Your look. Do you want it to
be fun? Nature-y? Sporty? Prom queeny?"

"How about something a little more **European?**" I said.

"European," mused Penny. "Like wearing lederhosen?"

"No, no. I was thinking French!" I explained.

"**Mais oui.** So, first things first," Penny began. "We need to do your makeup."

"I usually just do a little lip gloss and whiskerliner, but if you think—"

"You need to put on a LOT of makeup if you want it to show up in your photos."

I shrugged. "If you say so."

It was hard not to giggle as she began brushing my face with every kind of makeup known to mousekind: foundation, powder, blush, eyeliner, eye shadow, false eyelashes, mascara, lip liner, lipstick, lip gloss, and eyebrow pencil.

By the end of it, I wasn't even sure any of my "real" face was actually showing. But Penny was a master—and had 4,682 followers to prove it—so I decided to let go and trust her on this one. Besides, it would all wash off, right? **Right?**

Next came whiskers. Mine obviously needed to be straightened. Penny suggested we use her trusty straightening iron. I hoped it worked better than that straightening cream I used that made my whiskers fall off!

"Now, it's essential that you DO NOT MOVE at all once I start the straightening process," she warned me, moving the setting on the dial to HIGH. "The iron gets VERY hot and can easily burn you if you're not careful."

I nodded, closing my eyes as she did the first side. I didn't dare move.

"One ... two ... three," she said, releasing the clamp. "Voilà!"

I looked in the mirror. Wow, my left whiskers really looked great!

Is this what it feels like to be Felicia? I wondered.

Suddenly, Penny's phone rang.

"I have to get that," she said. "Do the right side in the meantime so we can get started on the photos."

I looked in the mirror. If the whiskers had come out this great on the HIGH setting, just think how great they would come out on the SCORCHING setting! I turned the dial all the way up, and slowly began straightening the other side of my whiskers. My eyes teared up as the steam came off the iron, and I could smell something yucky like burning rubber. I released the clamp immediately.

"AHHHH!!!" I screamed.

Penny came running back into the room with phone in hand. "What?! Are you okay?" she asked. "Did you burn yourself?!"

"No," I said. "But my whiskers burned right off!"

Penny's face changed from worried to amused. Then she started cracking up.

"Don't worry," she said, turning off the straightener and unplugging it. "We can use my computer program to add them back in."

Now for the most important part of all: wardrobe!

Penny and I raided her closet, trying on all different dresses, shirts, skirts, and pants until we arrived at the Frenchiest outfit of all: a black skirt with a striped Parisian boatneck top, a cute little beret, and a fashion scarf around my neck.

"**Ooh la la,** Babymouse!" Penny said. "You look **magnifique!**"

Finally, I was ready for my close-up!

"Now, we should start by relaxing and stretching your face muscles so you can smile properly. Do what I do."

She smiled as widely as she possibly could, showing all her teeth and moving her chin backward and forward, up and down. She then moved her lips from side to side so much that I thought they might fall off her face. Next, she moved her eyebrows and forehead right, left, up, and down.

Who knew there was so much prep work to get a natural smile?

After ten more minutes of practicing my smile, Penny announced that I was looking good.

"Let's get started," she said.

She looked through her camera and started snapping.

"Give me a bunch of different looks," she told me.

When we were all done, Penny uploaded the images to her computer. We picked out the shot I liked the best, and Penny went into editorial mode.

"This is what they do with the images of models in fashion magazines," she explained.

She began airbrushing, tweaking, lightening, darkening, and slimming until she had everything absolutely perfect.

I couldn't believe it! I looked just like a model!

I couldn't BELIEVE how fabulous I looked.

"Penny, you're a genius!" I told her as I uploaded my new profile pic to the SoFamous app.

"Magnifique!" she replied, giving me a high five. We treated ourselves to a chocolate milk to celebrate our success.

Suddenly, my phone rang. Was it a talent agency? Modeling scout? Every person who had ever been mean to me calling to apologize and beg for my forgiveness?

I looked down. It was Gramps.

"Hello?" I answered.

"Babymouse! Someone hacked your SoFamous account! They just uploaded a photo of a strange Frenchwoman to your profile."

"That's **me**, Gramps," I said.

Le sigh.

App-titude

By the time Monday rolled around, I was happy to go back to school because I still felt so glamorous. Sure, it had taken a half hour to remove all the makeup when I got home from Penny's, but it was a small price to pay for all the fun we had and how beautiful I felt.

RINGGGG!

Time for gym class.

We all changed into our totally NOT

magnifique gym uniforms and filed into the gymnasium.

Our gym teacher, Ms. DiMaggio, blew her whistle. "All right, everyone. Today we're going to take a break and watch a movie."

Everyone cheered.

"Just kidding!" she continued. "We're running laps. Start stretching."

We got down on the floor mats and began to stretch.

I groaned. "I hate running laps."

"Running laps isn't so bad with the GymIsSuperFun app," Georgie whispered next to me, showing me his phone.

"What's that?" I asked.

"It's an app that tells you how fast you're running," he replied.

"Cool!"

"Babymouse! Georgie!" Ms. DiMaggio yelled. "Less talking, more stretching!"

I thought about what Georgie had said

as I struggled to reach my toes. I still had barely any apps on my phone.

"What other apps do you have, Georgie?" I whispered.

"Hmm. Well, if you're talking about health and fitness, you can also get BreatheApp. It tells you if you're breathing. And BloodApp, which tells you if your blood is flowing. And BrainApp, which tells you if your brain is thinking."

"So, basically, these apps tell me if I'm ALIVE?"

"No, no. That would be AliveApp. Totally different. That's a premium app you pay for."

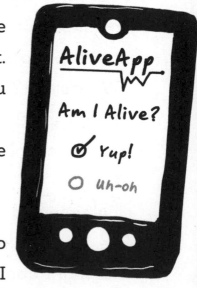

I needed to get these apps ASAPP! Er, ASAP.

By the time I got back to the locker room, I felt like I

was going to collapse. I decided to catch my breath while I looked at some other apps. I pulled up the Whiz Bang™ app shop on my phone but was immediately overwhelmed by choices.

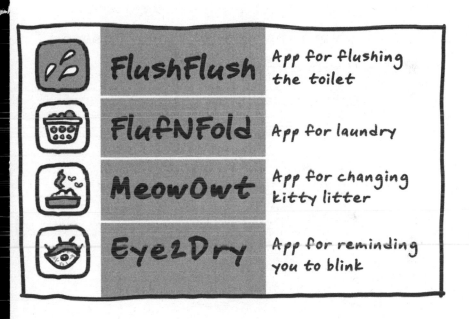

	FlushFlush	App for flushing the toilet
	FlufNFold	App for laundry
	MeowOwt	App for changing kitty litter
	Eye2Dry	App for reminding you to blink

Felicia looked over my shoulder.

"I know what app you should get, Baby-mouse," she said.

"Really? Which one?" I asked.

"An app for perfect whiskers!" Felicia said.

Argh. That made me mad. But also kind of curious about whether that was a real thing. . . . I would have to look into it once my whiskers grew back.

Later that day, I was at my locker between classes when I got a random text. It was the unidentified texter again! I shook my head in frustration. I still had no idea who it was!

I couldn't believe it! (Not about that sandwich. **That** I could believe.) MY PHONE WAS GONE. It was tragic. My mind raced through all the magical moments we had had together, like a montage. (A very short montage, but still . . .)

NOT A SINGLE ONE OF THOSE THINGS EVER HAPPENED, BABYMOUSE.

BE QUIET!

I'M HAVING A MAGICAL MOMENT!

I was already having separation anxiety. What would I do? And more importantly, what would I tell my parents?

As soon as I got home, I went on my computer to see if I could find an app to find a lost phone.

Free

Two days had passed, and I still couldn't find my phone. And what was worse—the apps that find your phone apparently only work if you download them BEFORE you lose it. What is the point in that?

HOW COULD I LIVE WITHOUT A PHONE?! (Well, except for all the time in my life I had previously lived without a phone....)

I had to get a new one ASAP. I would just have to come clean to my parents and beg for forgiveness.

My mom was at her desk.

"Mom, can I talk to you?" I asked.

"Sure, what's up?" she replied.

"What would you do if you lost something that was very expensive, and very important to you, and that you promised not to lose in the first place?" I figured if I kept it vague, she wouldn't suspect anything.

"You lost your phone already?" she asked.

How could she possibly know? I swear she was a mind reader!

"I think my locker ate it," I admitted.

"That's disappointing, Babymouse. Having a phone is a big responsibility. If you want a new one, you'll have to pay for it yourself."

Le sigh.

I logged on to the computer to take a look at my bank balance.

Account Balance

-$15.00

BANK ACCOUNT IN OVERDRAWN STATUS!

Ugh. It was worse than I thought, but I'd have to figure something out. I was going crazy without my phone. My fingers were shaking. My hands and heart felt so empty. (I had been secretly carrying around my calculator just to have something to keep me company. I think that remote-control experiment really messed with my head.)

I opened a new tab, and typed in the Whiz Bang™ website to see how much a new phone would cost.

Whiz Bang™   Features   Buy

The new Whiz Bang™
Oversize Mini

Big.
Sorta.

Get yours now **FREE*!**
Click here to find at
a retailer near you.

*New customers only.
*With a 32-month contract.
*Taxes and fees may apply.

FREE! Now, **that** I could afford!

I begged my mom to take me to the store. She agreed, but only after I promised to finish my homework and clean my room. I don't think I've ever been so excited to do my chores.

☆ ♡ ☆

My mom took Squeak and me to the Whiz Bang™ store later that night. Just my luck, the exact same employee was working.

"Hey! I remember you," she said. "Weren't you just here?"

"Yes," I replied, embarrassed. "I lost my phone, and I need a new one."

"Well, I'm sorry to hear that, but the good news is we have lots of exciting new models that came RIGHT AFTER you purchased your last phone!"

"New models? Oooh! Tell me more!"

"We've just introduced the new Whiz Bang™ **Oversize** Mini," the saleswoman said.

"I'll take it!"

"A Whiz Bang™ Oversize Mini?" my mom asked. "So it's a larger version of the Mini? Wouldn't that just be the same as the original?"

The saleswoman and I both had a good laugh. Mothers can be so embarrassing sometimes.

"Ma'am, these are completely different models," she explained. "The Whiz Bang™ Oversize Mini is larger than the Whiz Bang™ Oversize Mini Mini but not quite as large as the Whiz Bang™ Oversize Oversize Mini. Let me show you."

She pulled out a tray from under the counter.

"See, Mom." I pointed to their various awesome features. "They are all **totally** different."

"Whatever you say, Babymouse," she said. "It's your money, so it's up to you."

Here was my chance to impress everyone with my online research and savvy as a consumer. I picked out the Whiz Bang™ Oversize Mini, which was the one I had wanted originally.

"What color would you like?" the saleswoman asked.

"Do you have pink?"

"Do we have pink?" she laughed. "Of course we have pink! We have pink pink, off-pink, sunrise pink, sunset pink, flamingo pink, pink champagne, and bubble gum pink."

"Bubble gum, please." I wanted to keep it classic. Old-school pink.

"How much is it?" my mom asked.

"Great news!" continued the saleswoman.

"We're running a special right now, so your total is the low, low price of ninety dollars." Then, under her breath, she added, "Excluding taxes and fees, of course."

"Ninety dollars?! But the website said it would be free," I said, shocked.

"Oh, you must not have read the fine print. The phone is free only for new customers with a thirty-two month contract," she said. "You already have a contract with us, and you aren't due for an upgrade for at least another year."

Argh. That definitely complicated things.

"If you don't have the money, Babymouse," Squeak said, "I could lend it to you."

"That's so sweet, Squeak!" Mom said. "What a nice thing to do for your sister."

As it turned out, the phone was over a hundred dollars with taxes and fees, which really makes me wonder why people say "talk is cheap."

Whiz Bang™
Oversize Mini $90
Salesperson fee $10
Store service fee $10
Box fee $10
Instructions fee $10
"Fees applied" fee $10

TOTAL................ $140

"Thanks for lending me the money, Squeak," I said. "So, what's the catch?"

"Let's just say there's some fine print," he said with a smile.

In the end, I agreed to let him borrow the phone and to do his chores until I paid him back. As if that wasn't bad enough, he also made me promise to give him fifty percent of my next Halloween candy stash.

Typical 😕 -$ 😕 -$ 😕 -$

It was annoying to have to cough up all that cash, but it felt GREAT to have a phone again. This time around, I wouldn't let my Whiz Bang™ out of my sight (even more than the first time)! And I was going to keep my Precious safe.

MY PRECIOUSSS . . .

So the first thing I did was go online to look at phone cases. I thought this would be a pretty easy task, but, boy, was I wrong! There were hundreds—maybe even thousands—of different cases! And each one had all these cool special features.

There were shatterproof ones, which were so strong that you could drop your phone off the top of the Eiffel Tower without it breaking. 😄 There were waterproof cases, which were guaranteed to protect your phone under ten thousand leagues of water. There were glow-in-the-dark cases, which made finding your phone at night a snap. There were Velcro cases, which could keep your phone in place in your purse or backpack.

They even had a phone case "glove," which stuck to your hand so you never needed to put your phone down. I seriously considered that one, but there were some pretty big everyday drawbacks, TBH.

Then there was one SUPER-AWESOME PHONE CASE that had all of the above, plus a small pair of scissors, flashlight, USB drive, can opener, key ring, tweezers, and nail file. And it had koalas on the cover!

Koalas!!!!!!

Who could resist such cuteness?

Not me.

BABYMOUSE, DON'T FORGET TO DOWNLOAD THAT LOST-PHONE APP.

KOALAS!!!! SO CUTE!!!

SIGH.

Viral

On the bus the next morning, I over-heard some older girls in front of me talking about videos that were trending online.

"Did you see that new SkaterBoi video on Tubular?" the first girl asked.

"It was so good! He's my favorite!" said the second. "I could watch his videos all day!"

"Yeah. It's crazy to think he went viral

overnight," said the first girl. "Can you imagine what that's like?"

"Seriously," said the second. "One day you're just a normal kid, and the next day you're a celebrity heartthrob."

"I hear he's going to have his own television show," the first girl said.

"Maybe he'll get a movie deal?" the second one suggested hopefully.

I hadn't heard of SkaterBoi, but if these cool older girls were into him, I should definitely check him out. I did a search on Tubular, a video-sharing site. It turned out SkaterBoi was a teenage skateboarder with an insane number of followers. (And I did a quick search—none were clowns.)

He had a bunch of silly videos of himself doing random things, like skateboarding down a busy city street saying "Hi!" to people. I looked at the comments section below that video.

SkaterBoi Says "Hi!"
6,539,022 views
472,621 followers

COMMENTS ⊕Add

💟 **Sk8rGoirl419**
OMG I could watch this all day!!!!!

Ⓛ **LuvSkaterboi4eva**
💜💜💜 #OTP

🐵 **FabFelicia**
MARRY ME, SKATERBOIIIIIIIIII #MTB

👄 **YursTruly927**
"Hi!" Bwahaha

🎟 **RockRollSkate**
Such an artistic genius. #Prodigy

😎 **BoiCrazy10101xo**
Can't live w/o u. Srsly.

Hmm. These girls were really into this guy. That gave me an idea. Maybe the best way for me to become popular was to do something silly, post it on Tubular, and go viral overnight, just like SkaterBoi.

SHOULD I FILM A VIDEO FOR TUBULAR?

BECAUSE YOUR LAST FILMMAKING ATTEMPT WENT SO WELL, RIGHT, BABYMOUSE?

It was true that I had some experience* as a film director.

*See **Lights, Camera, Middle School!**

So I decided to shoot a video. What did I have to lose, right? But I needed something to set me apart from the millions of other videos online. In the biz, they call that a "hook."

I spent the whole school day trying to come up with creative ideas.

HOOK IDEAS

1. Flash-mob dance with koalas

2. Hamilton sing-along with koalas

3. Vespa scooter ride with koalas (who can I borrow a Vespa from?)

4. Beach Party with koalas (who can I borrow a beach from?)

After a while, I decided I would follow SkaterBoi's example and record myself saying one thing over and over again.

But what to say? . . . Hmm . . .

I needed some inspiration. I wanted my hook to be classic. Old-school.

So I looked through my mom's photo albums. Some of them were from the previous century—the 1970s. (Talk about ancient history!)

One thing was for certain: people sure dressed weird in the olden days.

"Who's this, Mom?" I asked, pointing to a picture.

"That's your grandfather," she said.

"He was pretty groovy back in the day," she added.

Groovy? Talk about an old-school-cool word!

"Do you want a cupcake?" she asked.

"That would be **groovy**," I said.

And just like that, I had my hook.

Now all I needed was the perfect location to film my video. Without a location scout, I had to make do with places around my neighborhood—ones I could walk to pretty easily.

Once I finished filming, I made a fun movie. Then I created a Tubular account (BabymouseXO) and started uploading the video. I waited impatiently.

10% . . . 20% . . . 30% . . . 40% . . . 50% . . . 60% . . . 70% . . . 80% . . . 90% . . .

KNOCK, KNOCK.

Someone was at my bedroom door.

"Who is it?" I asked.

"Squeak," came the muffled reply.

"What do you want?"

He opened the door. "I want to borrow your phone."

"Not now, Squeak. I'm uploading a video to Tubular."

"Huh?"

Sigh. "It's a video-streaming site. You can make movies for people to follow."

"Cool!" he said, inviting himself right in. "Will you show me how?"

I didn't want to be bothered, but he had just lent me all that money for the phone. I reluctantly agreed and quickly went over the basics with him.

"Can I borrow your phone tonight?" he asked.

"Ugh," I responded.

"Please?" he asked. "Remember our deal?"

"Okay, but I need it back first thing tomorrow morning. I mean it."

"You got it," he said.

Instead of surfing the Web and texting friends, I treated myself to a good, old-fashioned night of pampering. I needed to look great for my big celebrity debut the next day! I daydreamed about how amazing it would be to become famous overnight. The celebrity endorsement and appearance requests would pour in.

Everyone would want me to come to parties, benefits, and award shows, just to stand in the middle of a sparkly stage with hot lights and say "Groovy."

☆ ♡ ☆

The following morning, I went down for breakfast.

"Good morning, family," I announced grandly. "Do you have my phone, Squeak?"

"Morning, Babymouse," Mom said. "I'm happy to see you're sharing with your brother."

"Right here!" Squeak smiled at me and passed over my phone.

The weird thing was, when I got to school, I immediately **did** feel like a celebrity.

"There she is!" I heard a girl say.

"I can't believe that's her," said a boy I didn't know.

People were whispering, texting each other, and snapping photos of me from all angles. It was exciting, but also a little **weird.** I guessed I had better get used to the paparazzi if this was going to become my new life.

Wilson was waiting for me at my locker. He waved me down frantically.

"Don't worry, Wilson. Even though I'm famous now, I will still make time for the little people," I assured him.

"Yeah," he said. "About that. You really may want to rethink that video."

"What? Why?" I asked. I'd expected people to be jealous, but not my own best friend.

"Take a look for yourself," he said, holding up his phone.

OH. MY. GOODNESS.

OH, YEAH!

I FEEL PRETTY! I FEEL PRETTY!

GROOVY.

LE SIGH.

☆ ♥ ☆

When I got home from school that day, I told my parents what had happened. They made Squeak delete the video and gave him a long talking-to about privacy and respect. At the end of that conversation, they made him apologize to me. But I was so mad, I could barely look at him. That was the end of phone-sharing privileges, as far as I was concerned!

Get Lost!

I was glad the next day was a Saturday. I was so embarrassed I didn't think I'd ever get out of bed again. Unfortunately, Mom had other plans. She popped her head into my room at eight a.m., while I was still under the covers.

"Babymouse," she whispered. I pretended I was still sleeping.

"BABYMOUSE," she whisper-yelled, peeking under my blanket.

"What's up?" I asked groggily.

"Your grandfather called," she said. "He wants you to visit. I think it will be a good distraction from . . . yesterday. Would you like me to drive you over?"

"I'll go," I replied. "But I can walk to his house myself."

"Do you know how to get there?" she asked.

"Yep!" I responded, tapping my phone. "I've got the brand-new Don'tNeedAMap app."

I got dressed, brushed my teeth and whiskers, and headed downstairs. Mom was in the kitchen on her laptop. Squeak was eating cereal. I ignored him completely.

"Do we have any croissants?" I asked, opening the pantry door.

Mom looked up. "We're fresh out," she replied. "Same goes for baguettes, crepes, and **pain au chocolat,** unfortunately. How about a granola bar?"

I hated granola bars, but until I had my own patisserie, I guessed I would have to make do.

Now, on to Don'tNeedAMap app.

DON'TNEEDAMAP

Next ↱

< Arrival: 15 mins

I started walking.

"Turn right in five yards," Don'tNeedA-Map app said.

Yards? That was weird. Usually I measured things in feet, but oh well. I did what it told me, and casually strolled through five of my neighbors' yards, incognito. I ended up on a dead-end street.

"Turn left in twenty yards," Don'tNeedA-Map app said.

Twenty yards?! Now, that was pretty crazy. I was far-enough away from my house that I didn't know the people who lived in these houses, so I wasn't sure what to do.

"TURN LEFT IN TWENTY YARDS!" Don'tNeedAMap app said again, more loudly.

Was it just in my head, or was the app getting **angry**?

I looked around. I didn't see anyone,

so I decided to just go for it. I ran as fast as I possibly could. Dogs barked at me from all directions, and a rogue sprinkler soaked the left half of my body. But I made it!

"CROSS THREE-LANE HIGHWAY!" Don'tNeedAMap yelled.

This app definitely had a personality. A cranky one.

I decided to reroute.

"RECALCULATING!" Don'tNeedAMap boomed.

I waited. Nothing happened. I pressed the button again.

"I SAID RECALCULATING!" it snapped back.

DON'T RUSH ME!

I didn't want to wait around all day, so I decided to try to figure out another way myself. I walked forward in the direction it had told me to go before.

Suddenly, the Don'tNeedAMap app sprang to life again. "GO STRAIGHT," it said.

Directly ahead of me was a park with a duck pond.

"GO STRAIGHT!" it demanded again.

I didn't know what to do, so I just listened to the app. A couple of steps into the pond, I decided this was ridiculous and x-ed out of the app.

Suddenly, my phone buzzed. It was a text. I looked around to make sure no one had seen me walk into the pond. Luckily, no one was there except for a handful of confused geese.

I deleted the messages in annoyance.
I had to get to Gramps's house!

Four hours later, I FINALLY got to Gramps's house. I was sunburned and sweaty and had goose poop stuck to my shoes. The only good thing was, I had been out in the sun so long that my clothes had finally dried.

Say What?

On Monday, I did my best to keep my head down and ignore the snickers from other kids, still laughing about the video.

I was relieved when I finally got to study hall, where I could get some peace and quiet. I had never been so excited to study in my whole life! (Don't tell anyone I said that.)

Luckily, Georgie and Penny had already

gotten a good table in the back. I plopped my books down between them with a thud.

"There's our hometown hero," Georgie said with a good-natured smile.

"Very funny," I replied, rolling my eyes.

"Don't worry, Babymouse," Penny said. "Many artists are misunderstood during their lifetimes."

"Oh, speaking of art, did either of you write down the language arts assignment from class today? I forgot."

"Sure," Georgie said. "Let me check my SoLazy."

"What's SoLazy?" I asked.

"It's an app featuring voice-to-text software. You just talk into the phone and it writes everything down for you. You never have to lift a pen!"

"So it's like having a personal assistant taking notes for me?"

"Exactly," Georgie said.

I liked that idea A LOT. Imagine never having to decipher your own crazy handwriting! This was the app of my dreams! Or at least my midsummer night's dreams. Ha!

(I mean LOL!)

I downloaded SoLazy immediately, knowing my life would never be the same.

Once it was on my screen, I decided to give
it a try.

"SoLazy, text Wilson, 'Bonjour!'"

Bonjour!

 Wassup?

"SoLazy, text Wilson, 'Just trying out my
new SoLazy app.'"

Just trying out my new
SoLazy app.

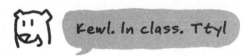 Kewl. In class. Ttyl

Just like that, I was OBSESSED!
☆ ♡ ☆

On the bus home from school, I had a brilliant idea: instead of typing out my homework, I could just **dictate** it to SoLazy!

The first thing on my to-do list was the language arts paper on **A Midsummer Night's Dream**. It's actually a pretty cool play by William Shakespeare about fairies and people and a love spell. And with SoLazy by my side, I got the paper "written" really quickly, which left me with plenty of time to watch the movie version. My mom found me on the couch halfway through my second cupcake.

"Don't you have any homework, Babymouse?" she asked.

"Already finished!" I replied proudly. "Just have to print it out."

Mom was impressed. "That's great!" she said. "So you can get to bed early tonight."

Argh.

☆ ♥ ☆

The next morning, I woke up early to print my paper. I connected to my wireless printer and opened my saved voice memo. I pressed the TRANSLATE TO TEXT button and waited for the app to update. Once that happened, I pressed PRINT and went to the bathroom to wash up. When I came back, I couldn't believe my eyes!

A Misnomer Right's Team

Bye Babymoose

I thought my problems would end there, but I was wrong. When I was at my locker between classes later that day, I got—you guessed it!—another text from "unidentified." I tried to use SoLazy to translate my messages. It couldn't be as bad as my paper (or so I thought . . .).

Man, was I frustrated. At first, it seemed like SoLazy was choosing the wrong words based on the app's algorithms, but then things started to get really weird. . . .

WHAT???

Photobomb

The texts from "unidentified" kept coming.

A stranger! On top of being really annoying, this person was making me break Rule #5. Enough was enough! I blocked the number.

Just then, Felicia and her pals walked by me, chatting.

"Felicia, is that the dress you wore on PA2ME?" Berry asked.

"Yes," she responded. "But I added the belt this time."

"It's totally swag!" Melinda cried.

"The swaggiest!" Belinda added.

Facepalm. ("Swaggiest" sounded like a word that SoLazy would come up with.)

But something about that conversation did interest me. What on earth was PA2ME?

Penny walked up a moment later.

"Hi, Babymouse."

"Have you heard of something called PA2ME?" I asked her.

"Sure, Babymouse," she said. "That's the nickname for the Pay Attention 2 Me 24/7 app."

"What's it do?"

"It's a popular photo-sharing service. People take pictures of things and post them online for everyone to see."

"Uh, what kinds of things do they post pictures of?" I asked.

"Like what you eat for breakfast," she said. "Or maybe a picture of your feet if you get a new toenail polish. There's been a lot of girls posting pics of perfect whiskers lately. It's pretty trendy."

I definitely needed this app.

☆ ♥ ☆

When I got home that afternoon, I created
an account on PA2ME. Now I had to docu-
ment something SO mesmerizing it would
make me instantly famous. Penny had
mentioned breakfast, so I decided to start
with a photo shoot starring one of Mom's
granola bars.

I uploaded the photo. Within minutes,
I had comments.

PA2ME

COMMENTS

⭐ **StarChildxOx:** So real. So RAW.

🙂 **MadisonC129:** It's like I'm seeing the inside of my soul for the very 1st time.

🏴 **EveryoneLovesMelinda:** UHHHHH I don't get it.

🌱 **Berryfull:** This pic is pretty "crumby." 😄

Eh, not exactly the reaction I was hoping for. I scrolled through some more images to see what other kinds of things people were posting. Quickly, I came to understand that the idea was to make yourself look good by showing off your friends, puppies, meals, vacations, etc. Basically, you got points for coolness by making other people **jealous.** I deleted the picture of my granola bar. Clearly no one was going to be jealous of that.

(Sorry, Mom.)

But at least now I knew the truth: I needed to make myself look cool by posting pictures of myself with OTHER people. Specifically, COOL people. And then I would be cool by association. That settled it. PA2ME was my ticket to being popular online. I would let other people make me cool.

And I knew just where to start.

"Felicia, can I take a picture with you?" I asked her the next morning on the bus.

"As if!" she snorted.

I guessed that was a "no."

Unfortunately, the only people who were willing to get pictures with me were not exactly going to elevate my social status.

"I'll take a picture with you, Babymouse," said Squeak. "But it's going to cost you."

Argh. The only person who would agree to be seen in a photo with me was my annoying Little? The sad thing was, he probably WAS cooler than me.

After school ended, I decided to stop by Grampamouse's place to see if he would be willing to help me out. I found him pulling weeds.

"Hey, Gramps!" I said.

"Babymouse!" he replied. "What a nice surprise. I wasn't expecting you today."

"I just wanted to stop in and see what's up."

"You know, the usual. Just some housework."

"Need a hand?" I asked.

"Sure! Thanks."

He and I worked on pulling up the weeds in his front yard. There were a lot of them! And I felt like every time I pulled one up, two or three more took its place. We chatted about the weather, our plans for the weekend, stuff going on in school, etc.

After a while, I decided to ask about the photo.

"Grampamouse, can I take a picture with you?"

"Sure, no problem."

"Thanks. It's for PA2ME. I need to add some photos."

"PA2ME, huh? That reminds me: look at the time!" Gramps suddenly got up and wiped his hands on his pants. "You know, I think we've made some really good progress today. I feel a little tired, so I'm going to head inside and take a nap."

"What?" I asked.

"I'll see you soon, Babymouse. Thanks for your help!" he said, giving me a quick hug and going inside.

I couldn't believe it. Not even my own grandfather was willing to take a picture with me?

Typical.

In class the next day, I couldn't concentrate. I was really getting bummed about the whole thing. My math teacher, Ms. Calculate, must have sensed that something was wrong.

"Babymouse, can you stay behind a minute?" she asked after class had ended.

I swallowed hard, gathered my things, and walked to her desk. I was worried I was in trouble.

"Is everything okay, Babymouse?" she asked. "You didn't seem like yourself today."

I wasn't sure whether I should tell her the truth. It seemed silly to say it out loud—that I was sad I wasn't popular on social media—but at the same time, my feelings of loneliness were pretty overwhelming. I decided just to let it out.

"This might sound silly, but no one is

willing to take a picture with me for PA2ME, and I feel really uncool and like I don't have any friends."

"Oh, Babymouse, you have lots of friends! I always see you in the hallways chatting with other kids. Lots of people like you and look up to you!"

"Yeah, it's just that on social media, I don't really have much of a following," I explained.

"Say no more. Look, let's get a picture of the two of us together. You can post that."

She and I took a selfie in front of the chalkboard, and I posted it to PA2ME.

"Thanks, Ms. Calculate," I said. "You're the best."

I guess a photo with our math assignment in the background wasn't "cool." As soon as I posted it, my score on the National Likability Index plummeted to -5,000,000!

(I told this to Ms. Calculate. But instead of being sympathetic, she was really excited and launched into an impromptu math lesson on negative numbers. Ugh.)

Getting a picture with Felicia was the fastest ticket to popularity. I had to come up with a plan to get a photo with her on the fly. I decided that if I just "happened" to appear where she and her friends were hanging out, I had a chance to stealthily photobomb her group.

"I wish there was an app that told you where people are all the time," I said to Wilson the next day at lunch.

"Like FiveCircle?" he asked.

"What's that?" Again, I was out of the loop.

"FiveCircle. It's a location-based app that allows you to 'check in' to various places, and also see where your family and friends are at any given time," he said.

"Perfect!" I exclaimed. "That's exactly what I need."

Wilson eyed me suspiciously. "You know, it's a little stalker-y, the way you just said that." He laughed nervously. "Do I need to be worried?"

"Not at all," I lied.

The bell rang, announcing the end of school. It was time to execute my POA (plan of action). I quickly packed up my things and headed out of the building. It was a nice day, and I sat on a bench near the track while waiting for FiveCircle to download to my phone.

Ms. DiMaggio was collecting hurdles from the field. She waved hello, and I waved back.

"Here to run more laps?" she teased.

"Not more laps. Just more apps!" I told her, smiling.

"You kids make me laugh," she said as she walked toward the gym.

Once she was out of sight, I entered Felicia's info into the FiveCircle database. A dial went around and around as it tried to locate her avatar. **Hurry up!** I thought frantically.

Felicia was still near the school! I sprinted back to the main entrance, where a bunch of kids were hanging out and catching up with friends while waiting for a pickup. It was crowded, but Felicia was easy to find, due to the high-pitched laughter coming from her entourage.

She, Belinda, Melinda, and Berry were sitting on a bench together, scrolling through pictures. I noticed a bush directly behind them. The perfect hiding spot!

I quickly threw on a sweatshirt from my backpack and flipped the hood up, covering my face. Out of sight, I sneakily made my way behind the bush to listen to their conversation.

"You guys want to come over this week-end?" Felicia asked. "My parents just got me a new flat-screen TV. It practically takes up a whole wall of my room."

"Awesome!" exclaimed Melinda. "We can watch some of my cousin's DVDs from the nineties!"

"Sounds good," said Belinda. "I'll bring the popcorn."

"And I'll bring the candy!" Berry added.

"Perfect!" Felicia exclaimed. "This deserves a photo op!"

That was my cue. As Felicia took out her phone, I peeked around the bush. I would be barely visible, but at least I would be in the picture.

Snap! I smiled at the sound of my success.

Shortly thereafter, the girls gathered up their things and left. I waited for ten minutes, then did another FiveCircle search for Felicia.

Friend Found!

Felicia Furrypaws is at the Coffee Shoppe, located at 101 Main Street.

Of course! The Coffee Shoppe!

I ran to it as fast as I could, slowing down a block or two before so that I could catch my breath. It was definitely a personal record.

Ms. DiMaggio would be proud, I thought.

I looked into the window and saw that Felicia and her friends were ordering drinks at the counter. I needed a way to get close without them seeing me. I waited for them to sit down with their drinks at their favorite table in a corner. It was weird to me that they liked that table so much, seeing as it was close to the bathroom. Maybe it was because they liked being able to touch up

their hair and makeup whenever they . . .
OH MY GOSH—that was it!

THE BATHROOM!

Felicia and the girls predictably took
their phones out to take pics of their match-
ing lattes. Right at that moment, I walked
in and hurried toward the bathroom. They
were too busy playing with filters to notice
me, so at the last second, I turned around
and popped my head into the frame.

Snap! Felicia took a pic with me in it.
Then I disappeared into the bathroom,
unnoticed. I did it!

I hate to admit it, but I hung out in the bathroom until Felicia's FiveCircle avatar moved to a new location.

Friend Found!

Felicia Furrypaws is at Glam Girl Nail and Threading Spa, located at 103 Main Street.

That was the salon right next door. I weighed my options. On the one hand, I could just go out the front door like a normal person and walk to the salon.

Or I could peek out the bathroom window and hope to get a glimpse of the girls from the parking lot side.

Yeah, this was more me.

I climbed up on the sink and peeked out the window. Sure enough, I could see

Felicia, Belinda, Melinda, and Berry through a window opposite me, sitting in pedicure chairs oohing and aahhing over celeb pics in gossip magazines.

That was it!

I walked out of the Coffee Shoppe and over to the salon. I took a deep breath and walked in like I owned the place. Chimes on the door announced my arrival, and, as expected, everyone looked up to see me standing there.

"Well, look who it is," Melinda laughed.

"Here for a pedicure, Babymouse?" Belinda asked.

"More like a pathetic-cure," Berry said, and they all burst into laughter.

"May I help you?" the woman at the front desk asked me.

"Yes," I said, trying to keep my voice calm. "I'm here for my weekly whisker threading."

"I see," she said. "Right this way, ma'am."

The woman had me sit on a large reclining chair, right across from the girls. I was a little nervous, as I had never had my whiskers threaded before. But could it be any worse than burning them off with a cream, and later with a SCORCHING-hot straightening iron? I guessed I was about to find out.

The woman leaned over me to see what she was working with.

"Hmm," she said. "It looks like you only have half of your whiskers."

I couldn't see the girls, but I heard them snickering in the background.

"Yeah—I—uh—" I stammered, trying to find words that wouldn't embarrass me further.

"You know, that look is very popular in Europe right now," she continued. "You're ahead of your time, my dear." I let out a deep breath of air I had not even realized I was holding in.

"And better yet," she said, "I'll only charge you half price."

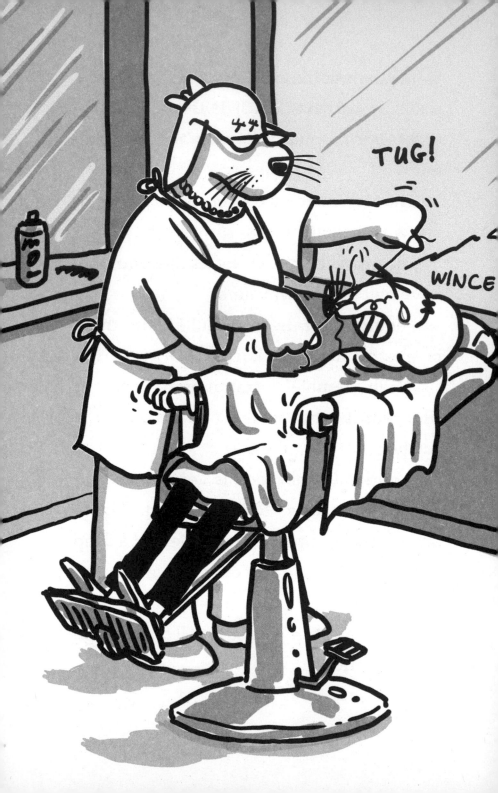

Now I was the one laughing. But that only lasted a minute before she began forcibly removing stray whiskers and I had to try with all my might not to scream like a maniac.

After a while, the aesthetician stopped so I could take a look in the mirror. This was pretty easy because the whole room was lined with mirrors.

"Let me know what you think," she said.

I looked into the reflective glass, but instead of checking out my perfectly threaded whiskers, I saw Felicia and crew getting ready to take a selfie. I smiled as they took the photo, fully knowing that my reflection was visible in the mirror behind them.

It scared me a little, how good I was at photobombing. But what scared me more was how much trouble I was going to be in if I didn't get home soon!

Fall of Rome

Home again, I hurried inside, kicked off my shoes, and dumped my backpack in the hallway. I needed to check all my apps!

Mom walked into the kitchen.

"There you are," she said. "I was starting to get worried!"

"Oh, you know me," I said guiltily. "Just enjoying some fresh air."

Mom walked over and took a close look at my face. "Something looks different about you," she said, puzzled. "Your whiskers look neater."

"Something like that." It wasn't **un**true.

"So how was school?"

"Not bad," I replied. "I learned a lot of new things."

"That's great! Like what?"

"Mostly about new apps and stuff," I replied.

Her smile faded. "I'm a little worried you're focusing too much on the digital world and not enough on the real one, Babymouse."

"Mom, I'm doing great in school," I replied. "I'm really on top of things."

It was mostly true, aside from the language arts paper fiasco.

"So your Rome report is ready to go?" she asked. "The one worth eighty percent of your final grade?"

I checked my phone. Sure enough, I had a "Report on Rome due!" notification in my Whiz Bang™ calendar.

"Yes," I said. "And you will be happy to know I actually finished it a long time ago."

"That's great!" Mom said. "I'd like to look it over."

"It's GONE??!!" I screamed. "What am I going to do? I don't even have the original handout the teacher gave us in class!"

"First, calm down. Then let's think of a solution, okay? Maybe a friend can lend you the worksheet."

"But I don't have any friends! Just look at SoFamous! I'm a tragic nobody!" I cried dramatically.

"Babymouse, you have plenty of **real-life** friends. Why don't you ask Wilson?"

Now, that was actually a pretty good idea.

do u have the Rome assignment?

I thought you were done.

I ran to Wilson's house as fast as I could (**without** the help of any fitness apps, I might add).

The gang was already there. They'd been working on their reports all afternoon.

"Hey, Babymouse!" Penny said.

Georgie waved, and Duckie gave me a high five.

I explained what had happened, and they were sympathetic.

"Rome wasn't built in a day, Babymouse, but it looks like your report will be!" Wilson told me with a smile.

Georgie showed me some cool sources on the Internet.

Duckie helped me with footnotes (and jokes).

We depicted the finer points of ancient Roman fashion. #TeamToga

Best of all, Wilson's mom made us delicious cupcakes.

Somehow it didn't seem as hard with all my friends around me. I got the project done (barely) and caught up on what was happening in everyone's lives.

"Thanks for having me over, Wilson," I said as he walked me to the door.

"No problem. We'll do it again soon."

He gave me a high five.

As I walked home, I realized how much FUN I'd just had. Which was kind of weird, because no one had used any of their devices the whole time.

That's when I realized that even though all those fancy apps were designed to make me feel more connected, they actually made me feel pretty LONELY.

I missed being with real live people.

That night before bed, I turned off my phone for the first time.

And it felt good.

#Typical

The next morning, I woke up with a start. My mom was downstairs yelling my name.

"Babymouse!" she called. "Are you awake? You're going to be late for school!"

I looked at my clock. It was eight-thirty already!

Eep! I'd overslept by a whole half hour. How had this happened?

BRUSH BRUSH STRETCH WIGGLE DRAG

MAYBE YOU SHOULD HAVE SET AN ALARM, BABYMOUSE.

BUT I TURNED OFF MY WHIZ BANG™!

I MEANT ON YOUR ALARM CLOCK. YOU KNOW, THAT ANCIENT PIECE OF TECHNOLOGY ON YOUR BEDSIDE TABLE?

ARGH.

I rushed to the bus stop, just in time to see the big yellow monstrosity pulling away.

"WAAAAAIT!" I screamed, chasing it down the street. My backpack was open, and papers, pens, and pencils were flying everywhere. Felicia and her friends were sitting in the back, watching and waving to me mockingly.

Georgie had craned his neck around to see what was going on. When he saw me running like a crazy person, he motioned to the bus driver to stop.

Moments later, the bus pulled to the side of the street so that I could get on. I was a sweaty, panting mess. I climbed aboard and mumbled, "Thanks," to the bus driver before collapsing into the seat next to Georgie.

"Sorry I didn't see you sooner," he said. "I didn't notice anything until I saw the video on Felicia's account." Ugh.

Penny moved back to sit by us.

"Want to borrow a brush?" she asked, handing me both a brush and a mirror. I did my best to freshen up and get everything reorganized in my bag. It was then that I realized the terrible truth: my Rome report, the one I had spent all night REdoing with my friends, must have fallen out during the chase.

"Georgie, let me see that video you were telling me about," I said, panicked.

He handed over his phone, and I clicked "Archive" and then "Most Recent." There I was on the screen.

It went like this: Me running awkwardly, shoelaces everywhere, with my glorious, most PERFECT Rome report flying out of my backpack like a dove being released into the sky by a magician. I watched as it flew gracefully through the air and landed in a big mud puddle, just as a camper rolled over it—PLOW!—smashing it into tiny, mushy bits. Then, more embarrassingly, there was me screaming "WAAAAAAAAAAAIT!" in slow motion over the sounds of a gaggle of nasty giggles from Felicia and her friends.

Tubular — Video — Crazy MouseBaby Chasing Bus

TUBULAR   Search

0:30

Crazy MouseBaby Chasing Bus
1,332,052 views
987,128 followers

COMMENTS ➕ Add
#1 FFFnumeroUno
Enjoy, my darlings!

Once I got to school, I went into the bathroom to take some slow, deep breaths before class. I was so angry! The first bell rang, a warning to everyone to get to class or risk getting detention.

I hurried back to my locker to get my books. On the way there, a kid I had never seen before walked over to me.

"I think this is yours," he said, handing me my report on Rome. The FIRST one.

I was in total shock. "You had my Rome report this whole time?!"

"I found it on the hallway floor a while ago," he said. "I've been texting you over and over again to return it, but I think you blocked me."

I was grateful but kind of annoyed.

"Thanks, but WHY didn't you just look for me IN PERSON to start with?? You could have just given it back to me a week ago! I had to write the whole report all over again!"

He shrugged. "My parents have a rule against talking to strangers, so I thought texting was better. Anyway. See ya."

Then he walked away.

I got to homeroom and took my seat just as the bell rang. People were talking about what was trending on PA2ME. I couldn't hear much of what they were saying, but one thing was clear. Kids were agreeing it was "hil-hair-ious!"

I pulled out my Whiz Bang™ and turned it on. I did a quick look through all my social-media accounts to see which one was blowing up.

#SquadGoals
#WhiskerBombed

#LottaLattes
#WhiskerBombed

#ManiPedis
#WhiskerBombed

Talk about bombing out. Maybe technology wasn't for me.

I DON'T KNOW ABOUT THE FALL OF ROME, BUT I SAW THAT FALL COMING A MILE AWAY.

GUESS I'M BACK TO THE SPIDER FILTER.

Le sigh.

Insights into Ancient Rome

By

Babymouse

Rome was an incredible civilization, although they had no Wi-Fi. Bummer.

For communication, they used men on horses who traveled from town to town, carrying messages. They actually built roads for the horses to ride on, which was considered a big advancement at the time.

Rome was ruled by emperors and the Senate. There were a lot of emperors over the years, and I think my favorite was Hadrian.

He had a cool beard (very hipster-ish).

While nothing can top French fashion (ooh la la!), Rome had a few good looks. They were big into togas and sandals. Togas were basically sheets that were draped around the body. They look very comfortable.

In terms of hairstyles, many men and women wore wigs in ancient Rome.

Dining was different from what we know today. People would recline on low couches to eat their meals. This had to be better than the cafeteria, in my opinion. And while there were no cupcakes (weep!), there was something called a honey cake, which sounds pretty tasty.

Chariot racing was popular in ancient Rome. It was a lot harder than just skateboarding, and I bet it would have even more followers today.

Romans spoke a language called Latin, which is apparently dead now, which seems harsh to me. (Who kills languages, anyway?!?!)

One common Latin saying was felix culpa. This translates to "a happy fault." This means that sometimes you make a mistake that turns out to be good in the end. I have personally had a felix culpa recently.

In total, ancient Rome was very interesting and sounds like it was a lot more fun than middle school.

#FelixCulpa

☆ ♥ ☆

About the Authors

Jennifer L. Holm and **Matthew Holm** are a **New York Times** bestselling sister-and-brother team. They are the creators behind the Babymouse, Squish, and My First Comics series. The Eisner Award–winning Babymouse books have introduced millions of children to graphic novels. Jennifer is also the **New York Times** bestselling author of **The Fourteenth Goldfish** and several other highly acclaimed novels, including three Newbery Honor winners: **Our Only May Amelia, Penny from Heaven**, and **Turtle in Paradise.** Matthew is also the author of **Marvin and the Moths** with Jonathan Follett.

BABYMOUSE
TALES FROM THE LOCKER

When Babymouse gets to middle school, she wants to stand out. So she joins the film club to write and direct a sweeping cinematic epic.

PRODUCTION
"Au Revoir, My Locker"

SCENE	SHOT	TAKE
3	4	1

Will making the film of her dreams turn into a nightmare?

JENNIFER L. HOLM & MATTHEW HOLM

BABYMOUSE

TALES FROM THE LOCKER

Lights, Camera, Middle School!